WILD WITCHES' BALL

By Jack Prelutsky

Illustrated by Kelly Asbury

HarperFestival®
A Division of HarperCollinsPublishers

In every size and shape and weight,

We witches came
to celebrate.

Ten tall crones
with moans and groans

battled in barrels
with bats and bones.

Nine queer dears with pointed ears

dangled and swang from the chandeliers.

Witches eight with mangy tresses
danced with seven sorceresses.

Witches six
in shaggy rags

played toss
and tag
with five
old hags.

Four fat bags took healthy bites

from parts of three unsightly frights.

There were witches
squeezed in every nook

whichever where
you cared to look.

How many witches can you see